MW01124642

Her Lover

by

Maxim Gorky

Rise of Douai

Copyright © 2014 Rise of Douai

ISBN-13:
978-1499595635

ISBN-10:
1499595638

1

Introduction

Alexei Maximovich Peshkov 28 March 1868 – 18 June 1936, primarily known as Maxim (Maksim) Gorky was a Russian and Soviet writer, a founder of the Socialist realism literary method and a political activist.

Gorky's reputation grew as a unique literary voice from the bottom strata of society and as a fervent advocate of Russia's social, political, and cultural transformation. By 1899, he was openly associating with the emerging Marxist social-democratic movement, which helped make him a celebrity among both the intelligentsia and the growing numbers of "conscious" workers. At the heart of all his work was a belief in the inherent worth and potential of the human person (личность, 'lichnost'). In his writing, he counterposed individuals, aware of their natural dignity, and inspired by energy and will, with people who succumb to the degrading conditions of life around them. Both his writings and his letters reveal a "restless man" (a frequent self-description) struggling to resolve contradictory feelings of faith and skepticism, love of life and disgust at the vulgarity and pettiness of the human world.

He publicly opposed the Tsarist regime and was arrested many times. Gorky befriended many revolutionaries and became a personal friend of Vladimir Lenin after they met in 1902. He exposed governmental control of the press (see Matvei Golovinski affair). In 1902, Gorky was elected an honorary Academician of Literature, but Tsar Nicholas II ordered this annulled. In protest, Anton Chekhov and Vladimir Korolenko left the Academy.

Leo Tolstoy with Gorky in Yasnaya Polyana, 1900.

From 1900 to 1905, Gorky's writings became more optimistic. He became more involved in the opposition movement, for which he was again briefly imprisoned in 1901. In 1904, having severed his relationship with the Moscow Art Theatre in the wake of conflict with Vladimir Nemirovich-Danchenko, Gorky returned to Nizhny Novgorod to establish a theatre of his own. Both Constantin Stanislavski and Savva Morozov provided financial support for the venture. Stanislavski believed that Gorky's theatre was an opportunity to develop the network of provincial theatres which he hoped would reform the art of the stage in Russia, a dream of his since the 1890s. He sent some pupils from the Art Theatre School—as well as Ioasaf Tikhomirov, who ran the school—to work there. By the autumn, however, after the censor had banned every play that the theatre proposed to stage, Gorky abandoned the project.

As a financially successful author, editor, and playwright, Gorky gave financial support to the Russian Social Democratic Labour Party (RSDLP), as well as supporting liberal appeals to the government for civil rights and social reform. The brutal shooting of workers marching to the Tsar with a petition for reform on 9 January 1905 (known as the "Bloody Sunday"), which set in motion the Revolution of 1905, seems to have pushed Gorky more decisively toward radical solutions. He became closely associated with Vladimir Lenin and Alexander Bogdanov's Bolshevik wing of the party, with Bogdanov taking responsibility for the transfer of funds from Gorky to Vpered. It is not clear whether he ever formally joined, and his relations with Lenin and the Bolsheviks would always be rocky. His most influential writings in these years were a series of political plays, most famously The Lower Depths (1902). While briefly imprisoned in Peter and Paul Fortress during the abortive 1905 Russian Revolution, Gorky wrote the play Children of the Sun, nominally set during an 1862 cholera epidemic, but universally understood to relate to present-day events.

Her Lover

AN acquaintance of mine once told me the following story.

When I was a student at Moscow I happened to live alongside one of those ladies whose repute is questionable.

She was a Pole, and they called her Teresa. She was a tallish, powerfully-built brunette, with black, bushy eye-brows and a large coarse face as if carved out by a hatchet—the bestial gleam of her dark eyes, her thick bass voice, her cabman-like gait and her immense muscular vigour, worthy of a fishwife, inspired me with horror. I lived on the top flight and her garret was opposite to mine. I never left my door open when I knew her to be at home. But this, after all, was a very rare occurrence. Sometimes I chanced to meet her on the staircase or in the yard, and she would smile upon me with a smile which seemed to me to be sly and cynical. Occasionally, I saw her drunk, with bleary eyes, tousled hair, and a particularly hideous grin On such occasions she would speak to me.

"How d'ye do, Mr. Student!" and her stupid laugh would still further intensify my loathing of her. I should have liked to have changed my quarters in order to have avoided such encounters and greetings; but my little chamber was a nice one, and there was such a wide view from the window, and it was always so quiet in the street below—so I endured.

And one morning I was sprawling on my couch, trying to find some sort of excuse for not attending my class, when the door opened, and the bass voice of Teresa the loath-some resounded from my threshold:

"Good health to you, Mr. Student!"

"What do you want?" I said. I saw that her face was confused and supplicatory. . . . It was a very unusual sort of face for her.

"Sir! I want to beg a favour of you. Will you grant it me?"

I lay there silent, and thought to myself:

"Gracious! . . . Courage, my boy!"

8

"I want to send a letter home, that's what it is," she said; her voice was beseeching, soft, timid.

"Deuce take you!" I thought; but up I jumped, sat down at my table, took a sheet of paper, and said:

"Come here, sit down, and dictate!"

She came, sat down very gingerly on a chair, and looked at me with a guilty look.

"Well, to whom do you want to write?"

"To Boleslav Kashput, at the town of Svieptziana, on the Warsaw Road. . . ."

"Well, fire away!"

"My dear Boles . . . my darling . . . my faithful lover. May the Mother of God protect thee! Thou heart of gold, why hast thou not written for such a long time to thy sorrowing little dove, Teresa?"

I very nearly burst out laughing. "A

9

sorrowing little dove!" more than five feet high, with fists a stone and more in weight, and as black a face as if the little dove had lived all its life in a chimney, and had never once washed itself! Restraining myself somehow, I asked:

"Who is this Bolest?"

"Boles, Mr. Student," she said, as if offended with me for blundering over the name, "he is Boles—my young man."

"Young man!"

"Why are you so surprised, sir? Cannot I, a girl, have a young man?"

She? A girl? Well!

"Oh, why not?" I said. "All things are possible. And has he been your young man long?"

"Six years."

"Oh, ho!" I thought. "Well, let us write your

letter. . . ."

And I tell you plainly that I would willingly have changed places with this Boles if his fair correspondent had been not Teresa but something less than she.

"I thank you most heartily, sir, for your kind services," said Teresa to me, with a curtsey. "Perhaps I can show you some service, eh?"

"No, I most humbly thank you all the same."

"Perhaps, sir, your shirts or your trousers may want a little mending?"

I felt that this mastodon in petticoats had made me grow quite red with shame, and I told her pretty sharply that I had no need whatever of her services.

She departed.

A week or two passed away. It was evening. I was sitting at my window whistling and thinking of some expedient for enabling me to get away from myself. I was bored; the weather was dirty. I didn't want to go out, and out of sheer ennui I began a course of self-analysis and reflection. This also was dull enough work, but I didn't care about doing anything else. Then the door opened. Heaven be praised! Some one came in.

"Oh, Mr. Student, you have no pressing business, I hope?"

It was Teresa. Humph!

"No. What is it?"

"I was going to ask you, sir, to write me another letter."

"Very well! To Boles, eh?"

"No, this time it is from him."

"Wha-at?"

"Stupid that I am! It is not for me, Mr. Student, I beg your pardon. It is for a friend of mine, that is to say, not a friend but an acquaintance—a man acquaintance. He has a sweetheart just like me here, Teresa. That's how it is. Will you, sir, write a letter to this Teresa?"

I looked at her—her face was troubled, her fingers were trembling. I was a bit fogged at first—and then I guessed how it was.

"Look here, my lady," I said, "there are no Boleses or Teresas at all, and you've been telling me a pack of lies. Don't you come sneaking about me any longer. I have no wish whatever to cultivate your acquaintance. Do you understand?"

And suddenly she grew strangely terrified and distraught; she began to shift from foot to foot without moving from the place, and spluttered comically, as if she wanted to say something and couldn't. I waited to see what would come of all this, and I saw and felt that, apparently, I had made a great mistake in suspecting her of wishing to draw me from the path of righteousness. It was evidently something very different.

"Mr. Student!" she began, and suddenly, waving her hand, she turned abruptly towards the door and went out. I remained with a very unpleasant feeling in my mind. I listened. Her door was flung violently to—plainly the poor wench was very angry. . . . I thought it over, and resolved to go to her, and, inviting her to come in here, write everything she wanted.

I entered her apartment. I looked round. She was sitting at the table, leaning on her elbows, with her head in her hands.

"Listen to me," I said.

Now, whenever I come to this point in my story, I always feel horribly awkward and idiotic. Well, well!

"Listen to me," I said.

She leaped from her seat, came towards me with flashing eyes, and laying her hands on my shoulders, began to whisper, or rather to hum in her peculiar bass voice:

"Look you, now! It's like this. There's no

Boles at all, and there's no Teresa either. But what's that to you? Is it a hard thing for you to draw your pen over paper? Eh? Ah, and you, too! Still such a little fair-haired boy! There's nobody at all, neither Boles, nor Teresa, only me. There you have it, and much good may it do you!"

"Pardon me!" said I, altogether flabbergasted by such a reception, "what is it all about? There's no Boles, you say?"

"No. So it is."

"And no Teresa either?"

"And no Teresa. I'm Teresa."

I didn't understand it at all. I fixed my eyes upon her, and tried to make out which of us was taking leave of his or her senses. But she went again to the table, searched about for something, came back to me, and said in an offended tone:

"If it was so hard for you to write to Boles, look, there's your letter, take it! Others will write for me."

I looked. In her hand was my letter to Boles. Phew!

"Listen, Teresa! What is the meaning of all this? Why must you get others to write for you when I have already written it, and you haven't sent it?"

"Sent it where?"

"Why, to this—Boles."

"There's no such person."

I absolutely did not understand it. There was nothing for me but to spit and go. Then she explained.

"What is it?" she said, still offended. "There's no such person, I tell you," and she extended her arms as if she herself did not understand why there should be no such person. "But I wanted him to be. . . . Am I then not a human creature like the rest of them? Yes, yes, I know, I know, of course. . . .

16

Yet no harm was done to any one by my writing to him that I can see. . . ."

"Pardon me—to whom?"

"To Boles, of course."

"But he doesn't exist."

"Alas! alas! But what if he doesn't? He doesn't exist, but he might! I write to him, and it looks as if he did exist. And Teresa—that's me, and he replies to me, and then I write to him again. . . ."

I understood at last. And I felt so sick, so miserable, so ashamed, somehow. Alongside of me, not three yards away, lived a human creature who had nobody in the world to treat her kindly, affectionately, and this human being had invented a friend for herself!

"Look, now! you wrote me a letter to Boles, and I gave it to some one else to read it to me; and when they read it to me I listened and fancied that Boles was there. And I asked you to write me a letter from Boles to Teresa—that is to me. When they write such a letter for me, and read it to me, I feel quite sure that Boles is there. And life grows easier for me in consequence."

"Deuce take you for a blockhead!" said I to myself when I heard this.

And from thenceforth, regularly, twice a week, I wrote a letter to Boles, and an answer from Boles to Teresa. I wrote those answers well. . . . She, of course, listened to them, and wept like anything, roared, I should say, with her bass voice. And in return for my thus moving her to tears by real letters from the imaginary Boles, she began to mend the holes I had in my socks, shirts, and other articles of clothing. Subsequently, about three months after this history began, they put her in prison for something or other. No doubt by this time she is dead.

My acquaintance shook the ash from his cigarette, looked pensively up at the sky, and thus concluded:

Well, well, the more a human creature has

tasted of bitter things the more it hungers after the sweet things of life. And we, wrapped round in the rags of our virtues, and regarding others through the mist of our self-sufficiency, and persuaded of our universal impeccability, do not understand this.

And the whole thing turns out pretty stupidly—and very cruelly. The fallen classes, we say. And who are the fallen classes, I should like to know? They are, first of all, people with the same bones, flesh, and blood and nerves as ourselves. We have been told this day after day for ages. And we actually listen—and the devil only knows how hideous the whole thing is. Or are we completely depraved by the loud sermonising of humanism? In reality, we also are fallen folks, and, so far as I can see, very deeply fallen into the abyss of self-sufficiency and the conviction of our own superiority. But enough of this. It is all as old as the hills—so old that it is a shame to speak of it. Very old indeed—yes, that's what it is!

THE END

RISE OF DOUAI

RISE OF DOUAI

TWITTER : @RISEOFDOUAI

- AN IDIOT'S GUIDE TO: BEE HUNTING BY JOHN LOCKARD, EDITED BY ARSALAN AHMED (2012)(PAPERBACK) ISBN-10: 1478383550

- THE RISE OF DOUAI BY ARSALAN AHMED (2012)(PAPERBACK) ISBN-10: 1479267783

- THE RICHEST MAN IN BABYLON BY GEORGE S. CLASON (2012) (PAPERBACK) ISBN-10: 1479377341

- THINK AND GROW RICH BY NAPOLEON HILL (2012) (PAPERBACK) ISBN-10: 1480061638

- AS A MAN THINKETH BY MR JAMES ALLEN (2012) (PAPERBACK) ISBN-10: 1480088161
- HOW TO ANALYZE PEOPLE ON

SIGHT BY ELSIE BENEDICT
(PAPERBACK) ISBN-10: 1480081272

- THE ART OF WAR BY MR SUN
  TZU (PAPERBACK) ISBN-10:
  1480082007
- MACBETH BY MR WILLIAM
  SHAKESPEARE (PAPERBACK)
  ISBN-10: 1480060682
- A CHRISTMAS CAROL BY MR
  CHARLES DICKENS ISBN-10:
  1481194755
- CREATING CAPITAL: MONEY-
  MAKING AS AN AIM IN BUSINESS
  BY MR FREDRICK L LIPMAN
  ISBN-10: 1481158996
- GETTING GOLD: A PRACTICAL
  TREATISE FOR PROSPECTORS,
  MINERS, AND STUDENTS BY MR
  JOSEPH COLIN FRANCIS
  JOHNSON ISBN-10: 1481090984
- THE INTERPRETATION OF
  DREAMS BY MR SIGMUND
  FREUD ISBN-10: 1481134558
- THE COMMUNIST MANIFESTO
  BY MR KARL MARX AND MR
  FRIDRICK ENGLES ISBN-10:

1480112445

- THE PRINCE BY MR NICCOLO MACHIAVELLI ISBN-10: 1480119601
- THE WAY TO WEALTH BY MR BENJAMIN FRANKLIN ISBN-10: 1480099651
- THE ART OF MONEY GETTING - OR GOLDEN RULES FOR MAKING MONEY (SUCCESS PRINCIPLES) BY MR PHINEAS TAYLOR BARNUM ISBN-10: 1480138622

Twitter : **@RiseofDouai**